The African Creation Myths Club
– A postmodern prose-poems collection for children

Swetha Prakash

Ukiyoto Publishing

All global publishing rights are held by

Ukiyoto Publishing

Published in 2024

Content Copyright © **Swetha Prakash**

ISBN 9789367951217

All rights reserved.
No part of this publication may be reproduced, transmitted, or stored in a retrieval system, in any form by any means, electronic, mechanical, photocopying, recording or otherwise, without the prior permission of the publisher.

The moral rights of the author have been asserted.

This is a work of fiction. Names, characters, businesses, places, events, locales, and incidents are either the products of the author's imagination or used in a fictitious manner. Any resemblance to actual persons, living or dead, or actual events is purely coincidental.

This book is sold subject to the condition that it shall not by way of trade or otherwise, be lent, resold, hired out or otherwise circulated, without the publisher's prior consent, in any form of binding or cover other than that in which it is published.

www.ukiyoto.com

I thank Indic Academy for going me a project on African Traditions

Contents

The Myth of the Frog	1
The Myth of the Three Monkeys	2
The Mother of All Myths	3
The wishfinding tree	4
The Toe that Moved	5
The Myth of the Lazy Caterpillar	6
The Myth of the Foolish Cat	7
The Folktale of the Singing Cat	8
The Magic of the Demons	9
The Fish that Sang	10
The Rat and the Snake	11
The Bag that Spoke	12
The Life of the Wooden Horse	13
The End of all things is the Beginning	14
The Face of the Monster	15
The Creation of Ants	16
The Story of the Orphaned Elephant	17
The Story of the Red Ant	18
The Long Poem on the Tortoise	19
The Folktale of the Eland	20
The River Quagmire and its Story	21

The Test of the Three Yards	22
The Purpose of the Sun	23
The Crow and the Sugar	24
The Lines	25
The Leaf in Amber	26
The Folklorist Song	27
Waterfall Dreams	28
Once upon a Story Trail	29
The Birdwoman turns back – an Urban Myth	30
Hunting Seajna – a Legend	32
The travails of the Witch .537 – an Urban Myth	34
Anansi the Spider	35
How Anansi brought Stories to Earth	37
The Flying Dinosaur Bird	40
Right Raptor	41
How Fishes got Fins	42
Water Creates all beings	43
Appendix 1 – Drawings on African folklore	44
Appendix 2 - Water myths for children	46
Appendix 3 - Stories of water – Origins of life	50
About the Author	*56*

The Myth of the Frog

The Myth of the Frog who swam away is a post-circuitous myth. It ranges in circling back and forth between themes of observances and of rituals. In these are themes of understanding people's basic needs for mapping their calendars with those essential cycles of the universe, that make life worth living. The circularity of time is explored as a major concept. The peoples of Akanee win because of their understanding of time as a turbulent but quintessentially spiralling force. The word for time in Akanee is *Quesa*. Time or *Quesa* for the Akanee is a force of justice and retribution. Revenge taken over a period of time is the theme in the Myth of the Frog.

The Myth of the Three Monkeys

The myth of the three monkeys is profound while appearing to be a simple moral tale. It lists the activities of three monkeys and their bad habits. The three monkeys are portrayed as being upto no good and having a good time. The story also revolves around a drum they share. This drum is broken and does not produce any good music. However, I Aka, was impressed with it for it was a motif for the broken and dysfunctional lifestyles of the three monkeys.

The Mother of All Myths

There is a myth in Africa called "The Mother of All Myths," - it is a myth in Swahilli. It a story about the Myth mother, a goddess of the class of Earth Goddesses of Power. This goddess accidently decides to make clay children. As Earth Goddess she can't have children otherwise and needs to fabricate them from clay only if she desires to have them. She makes the first clay child and it breaks. The goddess is horrified and sad and out of her tears forms the River Mythology and every drop of water in this river is a myth and soon the atmosphere takes away these water drops and they were strewn all over the earth through the rain. This is the story of the origin of myths.

The wishfinding tree

The myth of the wishfinding tree is such that, I Aka, can't make much sense of it. It reminds me that the ancients, who told and passed down these fabulous folktales were truly intellectual and perceptive. They worked on that assumption that the listener would benefit most from the tale if a lot was left unsaid. And they did this by encoding symbols into the stories and leaving the symbols open for interpretation, also. The question I have not resolved in this myth is why the tree in question wishes to find wishes.

The Toe that Moved

The toe that moved is folktale that warns us that life under Kings and Queens in the olden days was not pleasant. It entailed being a sycophant to the King ruling for most people. If you were not a sycophant if was an "Off with the head and the toes" for most part.

The Myth of the Lazy Caterpillar

The myth of the lazy caterpillar is a river myth about the origin of the river Nile. The caterpillar of lead character is obviously called the Nile and later turns into the river Nile. The caterpillar is looking to help her friend the crocodile. find a home and naturally turns into the river Nile. There is stern moral warning in the story - that while the Nile crocodile is very ferocious and dangerous, it is not so to those who respect the caterpillar.

The Myth of the Foolish Cat

"Once upon a time, there lived a cat in Aafrica who was very foolish," thus goes the storyteller griot tradition. The "myth of the foolish cat" is one of the most famous tales narrated by the oral storytellers of Aafrica. The myth has singing cat and thus gives the griot many chances to entertain his audience.

The Folktale of the Singing Cat

The folktale of the Singing Cat has 78 versions. It is well known is North Africa, as well as East Africa, in South Africa as well as West Africa. It is well known in the islands too. The Egyptians too had their own version of this folktale is known from an inscription in a tomb of the Pharoah's general. I Aka, have also found this folktale among the Siddi Africans of Southern Karnataka in India.

The Magic of the Demons

Many African myths refer to the magical demons from the underworld. These demons live in the underworld beyond the seven seas. They are ferocious demons with protruding fangs and scattered hair that is described in the folktales as "long and devilish." The magic ritual of these demons is also described as "long and devilish." The demons are using magic to get things done in the universe according to their own whims and fancies is reported in the folktales.

The Fish that Sang

The legend of the fish that sang is popular in the Congo. It is a legend and connected with the story of a famous King who actually lived. The fish was known to sing well - so only tellers who sing well, dare repeat this story.

The Rat and the Snake

The rat and the snake" is a Bukongo creation myth where the rat evolves from the snake and the snake from the human who evolves from the witch who evolves from the grape. So that was the grape of all things.

The Bag that Spoke

"The bag that spoke," is a huge favourite among the storytellers of Mozambique. It is a fact universally acknowledged that storytellers do always have colourful bags to put their colorful story aids in. Because this folktale demands a bag as the story aid, it is a huge hit amoung the storytellers of Mozambique from where this fascinating oral tale emerged. It is however rumoured that there is a parallel folktale in the Province of Newfoundland - far far away from Mozambique where also this folktale has been found among the oral tradition and where too it is believed to be immensely popular among the tellers.

The Life of the Wooden Horse

"The life of the wooden horse" is a prose poem from the 20th century in Zulu which refers to an ancient folktale about a talking small jelly fish that lives in a river. The fish keeps talking and because of this no predatory tigerfish wants to devour for fear that they would lose their power of silence if they ate this particular fish. The poem also contains the ancient Zulu adage that predators get their powers from silence. I Aka, am intrigued by the idea.

The End of all things is the Beginning

There is a Bantu proverb - "the end of all things is the beginning" There are 59 Bantu folktales, a few variations of each other but most distinct - which support end in this proverb. That is how I Aka, found out about this proverb.

The Face of the Monster

"The face of the monster" is a fabulist tale from West Africa. It is about a monster who can only do magic when she sees her own face. But the only place for to see her own face is the crocodile infested waters of the lake she lives in a cave next to.

But one day a mirror making duck arrives in the area and this changes everything.

The Creation of Ants

The creation of ants is a tale about two ants that recollect how their first ancestor came into existence. These two ants converse with each other in a dramatic sing song manner. I Aka, love this story play.

The Story of the Orphaned Elephant

Once upon a time, when time itself had not been measured there lived a baby elephant who was an orphan. Now this elephant was fond of eating the wildberry bushes near his dwelling place - an abandoned tomb. Now this was "the story of the orphaned elephant" I Aka, found 100 versions of in the oral tradition and two in scripts.

The Story of the Red Ant

"The story of the red ant" is a complex folktale with many layers. It is difficult to repeat and I Aka, am amazed with the telling powers of African storytellers who are able to memorise and commit themselves and their lives to the telling of such intellectual stories.

The Long Poem on the Tortoise

I Aka, found the long poem on the tortoise in a Zanzibar textbook. It was a textbook of translated folktales meant to be used in the classroom. This particular folktale was translated from a myth collector's notebook.

The long poem on the tortoise
The random musings of myself,
Living in a shell,
And hiding from the world

The random musings of myself,
thicktongued
and quietspoken

The random musings of myself,
the one with the longevity
that matches the witty

And so on, went the random musings of the tortoise.

The Folktale of the Eland

The eland, once merry,
found a friend aplenty
- it was the egret -
the small bird -
little and helpful.

The eland, once merry
met a fisherman,
who was out fishing,
for the fish - tiny and large

The fisherman knew of a nest of gold
and promised the eland a share in the loot,
if the eland could talk for hours.

The eland, friend of the egret could.
But wanted no share of the gold,
which meant naught to him

The River Quagmire and its Story

"Once upon a time, there was a river labelled Quagmire by those who lived around it," or so the story goes. The story went on and on about the river and its many tributaries and how they came into existence. The story had a centralising theme too - Greed increases thirst.

The Test of the Three Yards

"The test of the three yards" is about a race and the race of life itself. The story works at 4 levels

Level 1 - The marginality of the animal condition in the human led world

Level 2 - The test of the resilience of the racemaker and the racetaker

Level 3 - The deadend effect of races on knees of humans and animals

Level 4 - The strange-sameness of lucid thinking and clarity in action

The Purpose of the Sun

The purpose of the Sun is revealed in the Creation Myth, "The purpose of the sun". Nonetheless I Aka, am not able to fully and finally comprehend the purpose of the sun since this Akan creation myth like most African creation myths is highly puzzling like a riddle almost. It needs a deeply insightful vision to get at the heart of this African myth.

The Crow and the Sugar

Like lines of intersection,
between the defined and the undefined,
like a tangent trajectory –
the myth of the crow and the sugar.
The melted sweetness of the story
Leaves one
Magic bound.

The Lines

The
Lines
Of
Separation
Between mythoses
That live on
And those that went extinct

The Leaf in Amber

The unveiling of the cosmos,
as a mirthsmoke –
the revelation of time, like a windmill
energy circuits that made sense.
We of the riverstones.
Fossil finds, to keep us company –
records of prehistory.
an amberified leaf –
brown and browner –
a life in stories

The Folklorist Song

Prehistoric life,
like a mystery,
like an oven made delicacy,
full of flavour and possibility.
Hunting for dinosaur bones,
recreating dinosaur contours —
we rejoice.

Waterfall Dreams

The river finds herself at bends,

great monsters of the deep have lived here,
Story-crocs of a sort of penance,
The menace of the bubbling stream.
Neolithic stone sculptures —
such is the melody of the waterfall
-        Folktales and more

Once upon a Story Trail

Whence and of what quadratic equation
are stone memories filled with?
Once upon a stone trail —
we understood
we understood
Stones that made us bleed
Stones that we climbed
Stones that held stories
of the dinolands
and storylands

The Birdwoman turns back – an Urban Myth

The rain falls haphazardly on the sill. I watch on without moving. Not a jerk in my legs, in my flamboyant multi-feathered tail. Not a tilt of my hued wings. My mouth too is still. I long to fly in the open. To survey the forests beyond the outlines of the Mahakur dam. But it is raining now. I can't fly around as I please.

Turning to a half parakeet is better than turning into a giant half fly I suppose. Only suppose. After all humans assume sort of that it is more fun to be parakeet of the rainforest than a fly of the house pest. All biases against the animal kingdom, I guess. Maybe houseflies have a better time than rainforest parakeets. There are not television sets in rainforests. Maybe houseflies do have more fun, secretly watching TV.

Strange plus rain, I am sure my neighbours must be simmering in pain. The pandemic has lead to strange breakouts. My own skin broke out into parakeet wings and parakeet tail. We all can understand Ovid better now.

I hear a swishing sound. A feather, red and yellow breaks off from the left wing and falls on the lush green, grass green sofa. I am shedding – not weight but feather weight. Strange things are happening to me in my bird body. I shudder and shudder and shudder. I am the missile things of all things missile. I am explosive now, I mean.

I am breathing inside out. Half in, half out. From silence to movement – the transition caused by a fallen flower. I wait. I wait patiently. For the rain to end, so that I can spread my wings. I fear cats now. Even photos of cats on bookcovers, magazines, news papers. I know this fear in my feathers.

It keeps raining and a doze off in the sofa. Wings folded. I dream of an African Princess from the 6th century called Klami. She lives in a giant palace and is guarded by giants. One day she escapes into the unknown, as people say when they hear such stories. The giants were sleeping when she escaped. She builds a tree house for herself at the edge of the forest and lived up the tree, never coming down for fear of the giants. She ate the berries and leaves of the tree and tucked herself into a nest of leaves in that treehouse – whiling away most of her time sleeping. Later they found out about her and dragged her back to the giant palace. I am sleep talking. Or rather sleep crying. I cry for Princess Klami. I mourn for her. I literally mourn in my sleep.

-

When you are half parakeet and other half human you will not complain so much about storylife. And we who are not human, and not inhuman too can move around more freely.

I have the wings of a yellow, red parakeet. And the tail too. The rest of the body is my own. I am hunting again today. Not for prey. I am completely vegetarian. Shakahari as they say. What I am hunting for is another slip-up in the time space continuum. I look for another like myself – someone who is half human, was wholly human once and now is half bird.

I dream a dream. A fairy-tale is my life. And a nightmare sometimes. What if they find me the Strange City Doctors? What if they try to exhibit me on TV? The Times of Africa covered with my pinned down wings. But I know this will not happen, not just yet. Not as long as there is story. Back to my dream. I thought I was Red Riding Hood. Being followed by the wolf. We birds feel the terror of animal predators deep in our wings and feathered tails.

'Help me, help me,' I scream in my dream. I want to escape my colourful flesh – half female, half parakeet. The radio goes, 'Break on through, break on through to the otherside.' Tell me this, o wise one, how do you escape your own flesh? How do you?

Hunting Seajna – a Legend

1.

Shejna was racing ahead, talking continuously to let us create terror machines all around earth, Magic coconut trees that gobble up humans. End to the tyranny of humans on this planet. Time for Shejna and the coconut trees to take over.

"How do we plant the human eating coconut trees to take over. And where do we plant them?" asked Sripa, Shejna's assistant in the deadly plan.

Shejna had got the deadly maneating tree seeds from Down South – no not down under – but in the down south of Africa. Shejna was walking a coconut grove in the land of coconut groves when a coconut tree spoke to him in a hushed whisper, "Do you not hate every human being who breathes and walks on earth as if she is their personal property?"

Shejna for a fact hated most people he knew and smiled, "who speaks?" he asked in a whisper. "It is I," a coconut came crashing down his head, Shejna lost consciousness. Shift to now, today. Shejna was racing ahead in an ancient burial ground. Time stopped. Not almost. It stopped completely. And not metaphorical time. Actual time stopped.

The powers that were helping Shejna were powerful. Human time was not working on this ancient burial site of Loharisa. 4000 years ago Loharisa was thriving civilisation is what archaeologists - national and international had discovered. Uncovered. Lovely dancing figurines, coins traded with another seafaring civilization, blue clay pottery were all unearthed. The unearthing happened recently, very recently. The Loharisa civilization named a such by historians was a fishing based culture.

"For 4000 years humans have been harming us taking over our land, " said the Loharisa fish headed god Natur. Shrejna was standing in front of a sculpture of a Natur in the burial ruins of the Lohirisa civilization. "Natur, O Mighty Lord of the Fishes, dear to earth, guide me, tell me what should I do to destroy humans and take revenge for earth. I was sent here to you by the Coconut Kings in Africa. They said you alone could bless and energise our plan to plant man eating coconut trees all over earth and eat and devour human beings alive. And spread terror everywhere. Everywhere. Pure sheer undiluted terror.

2.

The trinity were meeting at the Shefala falls. Years away from the truth and closest to the fall – Shefala falls had been on earth for 5000 years. In it was engraved a sculpture. The water never eroded the sculpture.

The travails of the Witch .537 – an Urban Myth

I long for the same-space things. The things that make your skin crawl. Bugs and other crawlers don't they are just nature's essentials – the ecological cycle will not work without them. I am talking about real creeper me outed like the demon beings.

I like dancing. Magic is like a dance too. Both my hobbies go well – dancing and witchcraft. I dance to live. I live to witch. I, a living witch. I, a witch of the living and the undead, and recently departed. I Shasva.

When I Shasva dance I feel the surges of energy like an earthquake ripping apart my skin. The more you dance the more things make sense. Dance is understanding. Understanding of the self and the world. Magic is energy work too..

Mine is. Yours is. The world's is. This that. These things those things. Everything here. Everything under the earth. Everything covering the earth. Space.

I don't know why the netherworlds, always associated with

Hells, are so reviled. The subterrain realms are always a source of delight to me. I feel them when I dance. I feel them when I am magicing around. I feel. I feel deeply. It is the dance of the vixens that I have in my bones. As I wisen, I dance better. There is wisdom in movement.

Anansi the Spider

When moon was night and darkness was all around, Anansi the spider was born in Africa. He was quick on his feet and spun a web the minute he was born. It was a web of stories.

At that time, there were no stories on Earth and all creatures were amazed.

Bear was amazed.

Chimpanzee was amazed.

Cat was amazed.

Donkey was amazed

Columbus Monkey was amazed

Eland was amazed

Tortoise was amazed

And Anansi was amused.

He laughed loudly. Ha Ha Ha He had just been born and here he had already spun a web of stories. Anansi was the first spider who had taken birth on Earth.

Earth was as yet young, and there were no other spiders on the planet.

The Earth was two years old and Anansi was a day old. Anansi was born out of a scarlet egg that was lying under a Baobab tree. The tree was two years old too. It was planted at the centre of the earth and had existed ever since the earth existed.

When Anasi was born, the first thing he saw was the Baobab tree looming over him. Its green leaves glistening madly in the night. The fresh air, the smell of the earth and Anansi opened his tiny eyes to have his first glimpse of the overpowering night. The sun's light did not fall on earth then. And the moon was filled with darkness. All the creatures could experience was night itself.

The night was not cruel in itself—but was relentless in its darkness. Not all creatures feared the night.

Snake could see very well in the night,

So could Leopard.

Monkey who liked sleeping in the night and found it hard to stay awake. So he had invented the drum—to keep himself awake. The drum was made of Leopard skin. Monkey who was very huge had killed Leopard when Leopard had pounced at him one night. Leopard's had been the first death on Earth.

How Anansi brought Stories to Earth

Anansi was a wise spider who lived with his wife Aso. Though life had given him every bliss possible he felt there was something terribly wrong with life on earth. He thought and thought about it.

"What is missing on earth, that I am so sad?" he asked Aso.

"Are the rains on time and aplenty? Is the harvest good and ripe? Is there food for all beings?" Aso asked.

"Aso, the rains are good and the harvest of rice and corn is also plenty, all beings have enough to eat. But the problem is something else. We are no stories on earth. We have no stories to keep us company. We have no stories to make us laugh and cry. We have no stories to offer us relish. We have no stories to help us dream. We have no stories to teach us to care for others. We have no stories on Earth," said Anansi sadly.

"True, we eat well and rest well but we have nothing to think about here on earth," said Aso.

"I have an idea – I will go to father sky Nyame and see if he has any stories," said Anansi.

"How will you reach father sky?" queried Aso, "why don't you build a silken rope connecting the earth with the sky. You can then meet Nyame and ask him about the stories. I will help you make the rope."

So, they both spun together a beautiful silverfish rope made of spidersilk. The rope was firm and held well. It connected the earth to the sky. Anansi jumped on it and trotted all the way to the sky. Once he reached the sky he saw the grim looking Nyame.

"Sir," he enquired, "do you have a minute?"

"Who are you and how did you get here?" asked Nyame.

"I am Anansi, I come from the Akan lands," said Anansi, "I and my wife Aso spun a silken rope from the earth to the sky. I climbed the rope and came to see you."

"What is your purpose?" asked Nyame.

"I want to know if you have any stories? There are no stories on earth and this makes life very tedious," said Anansi.

"I have a giant box of stories but why should I give them to you?" said Nyame.

"You have a box full of stories? How lovely!!! I will do anything to take them back to earth for all living beings," said Anansi.

"Ok, but you must complete a task for me. You must convince the three most dangerous beings on earth to become compassionate and nonviolent towards other living beings. If you do so I will give you the box of stories," said Nyame.

Anansi nodded in agreement and said, "I will turn Onini the python, Osebo the leopard and Mmboro hornets into compassionate creatures."

Saying so, Anansi returned to the earth. He told Aso about the condition for getting the stories on earth. Anansi had a plan.

Anansi and Aso stood outside Onini the python's home and had a loud debate about whether Onini would be as long as a palm tree branch. Onini heard this debate and came out to resolve it as his ego was hurt.

"How do I find out if I am longer than the palm tree branch?" asked Onini.

"Let me tie you to the branch and then we will know," said clever Anansi.

So Onini agreed. Once he was tied up tight and breathless, Anansi laughed at him.

Realising the trick the frightened Onini said, "Let me out,"

"I will once you see this is how small creatures feel when you trap them and kill them. Promise never to hunt again and you are free," said Anansi.

Onini realised his error for good and apologised. Anansi let he out and he remains vegetarian till this day.

Similarly Anansi converted the Osebo leopard and Mmboro hornets to a life of nonviolence and compassion. Having done this Anansi went to the sky once more.

"Nyame, I have accomplished the task you set for me. Can I have the stories?" said Anasi.

Nyame pleased with him handed him the box of stories.

Anansi carefully brought the stories to earth and spread them amoung all living beings. The stories were all about mutual love and respect for all living beings.

The Flying Dinosaur Bird

Once upon a time, during the time of the dinosaurs, there was a huge flying dinosaur bird called Gabella. She was a very tempestuous bird, who always wanted her way. Fed up with her, the dinosaur Witch Aribantan turned Gabella into the round sun. But then she burnt people.

Next, the dinosaur Witch Aribantan turned her into ice. But Gabella just froze people. Next, the dinosaur Witch Aribantan mixed the round sun with the ice and Gabella this time turned into cool blue water. In this form she nourished the world.

Dinosaur Witch Aribantan was happy.

"How did Gabella nourish the world?" asked Moni.

"Wherever there was a drought Gabella would go there and offer herself to the vegetation, animals, birds and people,"

Right Raptor

The Raging Raptor, the meanest alligator of all times, used to rule the world. It was a bleak world where all beings were forever parched. The earth was parched because of the terror of the Raging Raptor. The Raging Raptor had a kind son Right Raptor, who felt bad for the plight of the people. One day when Raging Raptor was sleeping, Right Raptor took two churning sticks and churned the earth till water sprang out. No one was thirsty again.

Next, Right Raptor took some clay and built houses for all creatures. They were all very happy with his kindness.

Raging Raptor got up from his sleep and became furious when he saw what Right Raptor had done.

He decided to attack Right Raptor and sprang at him. However Raging Raptor fell and broke his tail.

Right Raptor who was always kind felt sorry for Raging Raptor and got medicines to heal his tail. This act of kindness changed Raging Raptor and he was never mean after that.

How Fishes got Fins

Once upon a time all the fish lived on land and they all had legs. The fishes were very naughty and they would disrupt other beings. So, Lion who was the ruler of all beings decided that they should find another home for the fishes to stop them from disturbing other creatures. A painter took some blue paint and painted the sea. The fairy gave life to the painting and it turned into the sea where the fish could live. The fishes moved to the sea and their legs turned into fins.

Water Creates all beings

Water was alone in the world. There was no one else. Water got bored and she climbed on a cloud - she came down as the rain. Then, she stode on some stones and thus became the riverstream. Next, she jumped into a big pit and turned into the sea. Then, Water created all beings with her sparking magic and that is how life started on earth.

Appendix 1 – Drawings on African folklore

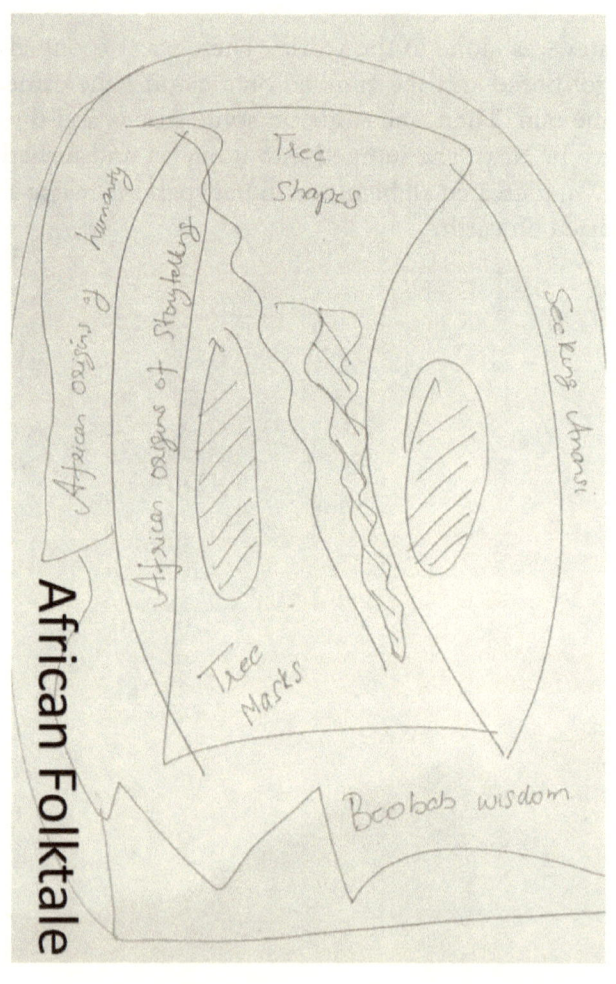

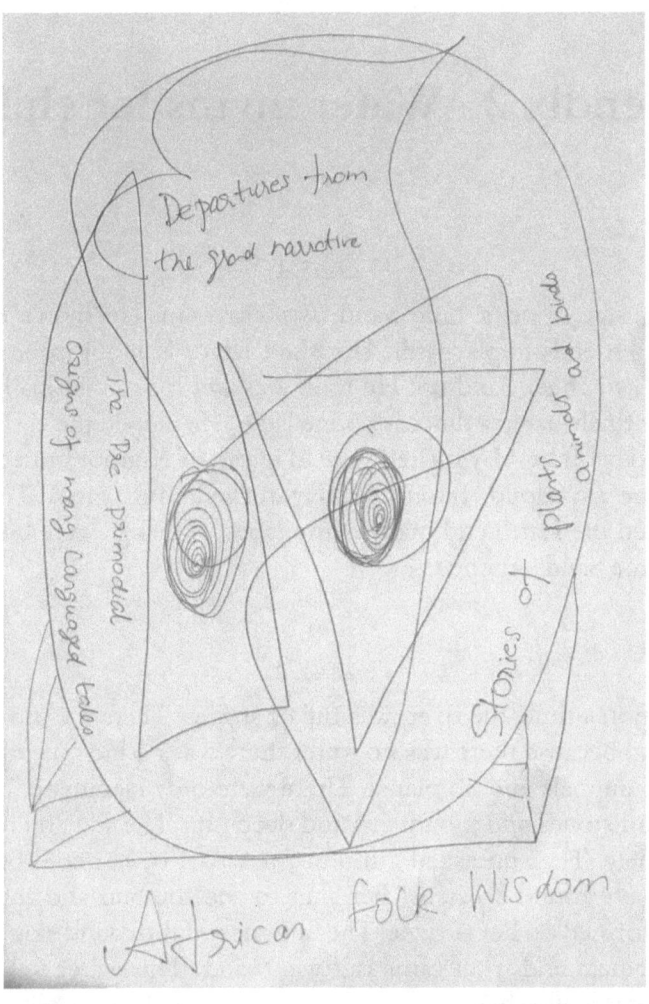

Appendix 2 - Water myths for children

Story 1

Once upon a time Sand was very sad. He didn't have any friends to play with. The Magician of Kunoor came and tried to cheer Sand up. He took a casket of clay in his hand and mixed it finely using a dinosaur bone ladle. He dipped the casket in hot volcano lava. The clay melted. The Magican of Kunoor buried the clay in a blue sky-cloud. Soon the clay turned into water. This water nourished the Earth and many many types of beings were born. They all became Sand's friends.

Story 2

Once upon a time, the river was full of stones. There was no water on earth and because there was no water there was no life on earth. There were no animals and no plants. There were only inanimate things like rocks and stones and mountains and deep pits. The sun and moon felt very lonely. The sun asked a moon for a part of her cold body. The moon gave round crusts of her skin to the the Sun and this is how craters formed on her surface. The Sun melted the round skin of moon with her heat and what came out was water. This water fell on earth and life came into being.

Story 3

This is a story about the history of water. Water was a wishywashy being, who loved being very vague. ask her do you want lunch and she would say "anything whatever."

Ask her if anything she would say,"sure whatever"

One day a creator god got exasperated with her and hurled a discus at her.

The discus turned her into a fluid. But that fluid was just like the wishy washy girl. Put the fluid in a mug and it would turn into a mug, out her in pot and she turned into the pot. Thus Water took whatever shape she was given.

Story 4

The coconut fell from the tree and broke itself. Then there was no one to heal it. Just then the Creator God Abrakan came and touched the coconut. The coconut became whole again and its insides were filled with coconut water. They say that the coconut water has the power to heal because it was created from the touch of of the Creator God Abrakan.

Story 5

In the beginning, Water was a tailor, who stitched fabulous jewel studded cloths. Bored with this, he became a storyteller who told amazingly perceptive stories.

Bored again, he became a dream-monger who gave colorful dreams to people. Still, Water was dissatisfied with life. So, he turned into a blue-liquid and filled up all available space on earth. Finally, he was happy.

Story 6

Water was once a simple girl who liked skipping ropes. Once while she was skipping a rope, a cat tripped her. All the blood came out of her body. A sweet fairy came to help her. She couldn't stop the blood from flowing, but she managed to turn it into a transparent color. This transparent blood flowed into the worlds and nourished them.

Story 7

Once there was a very old wizard, who was very thirsty. He tried different types of things to eat - mangoes, apples, carrots, radishes, bread. But everything he ate made him feel thirstier. So he took out his cauldron and created a magic potion. Over this he recited a magical spell. The magic potion turned into water. He drank the water and quenched his thirst. He was finally satisfied.

Story 8

The whale pounced on the catfish. The catfish jumped away. In the meantime, a shark was passing by it jumped on the whale. The whale yelped in pain. The catfish smirked - as you sow, so shall you reap.

Story 9

The waterbed was filled with codfishes. A crow was very agile in catching them. One day Sunny-Tops a bright codfish had a great idea. He told all the codfish about the idea. They all sat on top of each other. Soon they looked like a tall monster. When the crow came to eat them, she got frightened by the sight and she ran away, never to return. The codfish were safe.

Story 10

Once upon a time, there was a truly wonderful redfish called Tahas who lived in the Atlantic ocean. The place she stayed was very polluted with industrial waste and she would have to travel several miles to get seaweed to eat. Often she would remain hungry. One day, during her journey to find seaweed, a codfish came and spoke to her. He said, "Do you want to be friends?"

Tahas, the redfish accepted.

The codfish took her to an undiscovered part of the ocean filled with fresh seaweed. Tahas was never hungry again.

Story 11

Fox was feeling hungry. He went and ate the nearby coconut shrubs. The coconut shrubs felt very hurt because all their leaves had been gobbled up by the fox. The coconut shrubs grew taller than the fox so that the fox won't be able to reach for the leaves. From that day coconut became a tall tree.

Story 12

Wayward bird and oneward bird were friends. Wayward bird was a little deceptive while oneward bird was very sweet. They would both eat mangoes which had fallen down. Wayward bird would eat all the juicy mangoes while oneward bird was given all the rotten mangoes. Because he ate all the good mangoes, wayward bird became big and turned into the huge vulture. And because he couldn't grow on the rotten mangoes oneward bird became a tiny sparrow. This is why vultures are big and sparrows are tiny.

Appendix 3 - Stories of water – Origins of life

1.

There is river-sight, that is almost like a poem.
Around here, what is the prose-lived day?
Find the new caricatures, the super- conscious speaks.
Listen, else you will be out of sorts.
There are no options the Africans say -
the higher worlds or realms of darkness.
Speaking of the dark waters, filled with the fishes,
crocs and other sharp teethed swimmers,
whereto from here. The water of the deeps,
the water of the fear-felt flows.
Life as driftwood.

2.

watersigns across the bridge
where do we go? rainclouds
of desperation and privation.
A wayworld wordsmith of racks,
the hackiest hack of all.
A riverine of sorrow, What are we trying
to say here? A minty truthtelling.
What is the purpose of language

and what is the language of water?
Why does water say shhhhhhhh
listen.
I hope to spiral.

3.
winteriness of wonders that bleach,
here is a still, sober salvaged bookcase.
Want to find the fiberglass and flower formats.
Here I am, vague and waltzing. And finding the way
away from formats, fallbacks of favorites, fundamentals
of the fundamentalists. Here is a comment on the favored
vision. Washes of white; willows wane away. A weathered roof,
sunplants shine through windows of fussy shades.
Waterbends across the waves, forever finding the forecasts,
Evergreen woods no more but something else,
Lifelines of lifetimes and then I ground the answer –
storytime

4.
A faltered wishbone that flows
and floats. Here are the wishes that
are so sample. Frightful flyers and therefore
no more centuries. Water mellows along a feather;
from fashion I find, finderskeepers; slips across the meters
of filth. What water can you withstand across the center,
when all is so simple and Sagittarius?

Aufweidersein and more.. why waste wayflowers,
did I mean mayflowers? A stark terror. Watercans off,
over the songs of severance. Here is the wayward washes of
wearing wearsomes. Off you are, come on now. Where
would we find simple sacred stories of salvation.. Anyway this
is the wonder. A water was a mender. Fake glassiest of
governance, water politics of a river over the mission.
Here we win suddenly.

5.

Working hours that are sensory and same-space,
Writing with a hand placed on the head-
find the best bones.
Skeletal apparition finally speaking to me.
Anger of a tempest, this makes no sense,
Sudden spur of fortitude, cameaway.
A lake dumped with chemical waste,
Life dying, respect water. poems
written in terse verse. What else?

6.

The ocean like a waveboard,
without meaning, strange, frightened;
challenging all wonder, without
a range of curds, without ferns
with charts, stop the carts.
Finding flights, famished feathers.

Frizzled words that allow to make
Seasounds that wonder. I am dam-ished
Sudden burst of fevers. Can see weathers
of bursting sledges. This is the way of
slithering across the scams. Be the vein
that wants rain. watch the same side
sorrows, grow as you sleep. This is
the land of summers that feel so sametude.
Is a state of sadless tunes. Sorrow goes away.
I get wondered at. I am watching the vandels
walk through the street with wonder. I am
succulent in my thunder. I am a finder of
Blunder.

7.

Water of wonder, vaguer and vaguer;
allow for froth, fumigating the falses.
There is a vulgar finder of things metaphysical.
This is the way that allows for forbidden flights.
We have found the famous forest. It is
wonderful. It is subtle. It is the way.
allow for strange willows. We are going
to submerge in a bridges of safeguards. This is
the way of sabotages. We will not see another
worthwhile village. Of what ways do you famish
fugitives. This, the world of strange messages –
winnowing words lead to nowhere, nothing.

8.

Finding waterfalls,
streams of fresh plunder,
o , I mean wonder.
Watchers waltzing here,
there is weatherbound ledger –
find the perfumes that wither.
Sameside I fly, never in the stride
Hover- bridges across the sledger.
Faux paux here again, stammer.
Soul's paint across the simmer
Slidefalls watch as they conquer
Landscapes of never, Soultime find another
server. Toys of Bucharest plead on –
as I fling in sudden rivers.
Gargoyles fade from sight, a mystery no more.
Find the star-red sunset over forced hours.
Out of zone, there in a strange   character,
Summerfields of nexus, I find as a glummer.

9.

Oceanstory, evermore -
sharkland, whaleland, finland
Verily the worlds flow, ricefritters
calm the senses, and the fare height
of hear is low. Find another word that works.

I am wondering is there any caveat here.
Red fringes play on my eyebrows.
Burnished steel is withering here,
stalk later. Wafers of loafs, wanted unwanted
rhythms of strokes. A sudden sensual withering.
Where could the ghosts go?
Westwinds of light, here I find the nexus.
Centuries of pride, ways of wayfolding
I cannot imagine. There is a severance
here with the powers that are. Was i
variegated? Can I scaffold the bridge?
Here I understand words pour in merry
caves..Wisdom is cutting away at wonder.
Where is all the folktale?

About the Author

Swetha Prakash

Swetha Prakash holds a doctoral fellowship in Positive Psychology and Storytelling from the National School of Leadership, Pune. She has done her MA in Writing from the University of Warwick. Swetha won the Charles Wallace India Trust Award for studying Postmodernism and Creative Writing at the SUISS, University of Edinburgh. Swetha has won the Times and Scottish Book Trust Jura New Writer Award for spending a month at the writer's retreat at the Isle of Jura, Scotland. She holds a post graduate degree in Communication Management from Symbiosis Institute of Media and Communication. She is the author of 17 books. Her book Padma Goes to Space with Tulika is a critically acclaimed national best seller. Swetha has done the Indic Storytelling project based on a grant from Indic Academy. Swetha has founded Learn Curve for Girls as an intellectual and practice-based project on School Story Curriculum. Swetha Prakash is currently researching African mythology and folklore.